HAPPY and MAX

The Night in the Tree House

Story by Kris Jamsa, Ph.D.

Illustrations by Art Vandeleigh

Happy and Max
The Night in the Tree House

Story by Kris Jamsa, Ph.D.
Illustrations by Art Vandeleigh

...a young reader's best friend[tm]

ISBN 1-884133-89-4

Jamsa Press
2975 South Rainbow Suite I
Las Vegas, NV 89102
www.jamsa.com

For information about translations and product licensing of books in
the Kids Interactive Happy and Max series, please write to
Jamsa Press, 2975 South Rainbow Suite I, Las Vegas, NV 89102.

Printed in the USA 98765432

For information on other books in the Kids Interactive Happy and Max
series, visit our Web site at *www.HappyAndMax.com*.

This Happy and Max
Adventure Belongs To

_____

_____

_____

_____

Meet Happy, Max, and Trixie

Happy

Max

Trixie

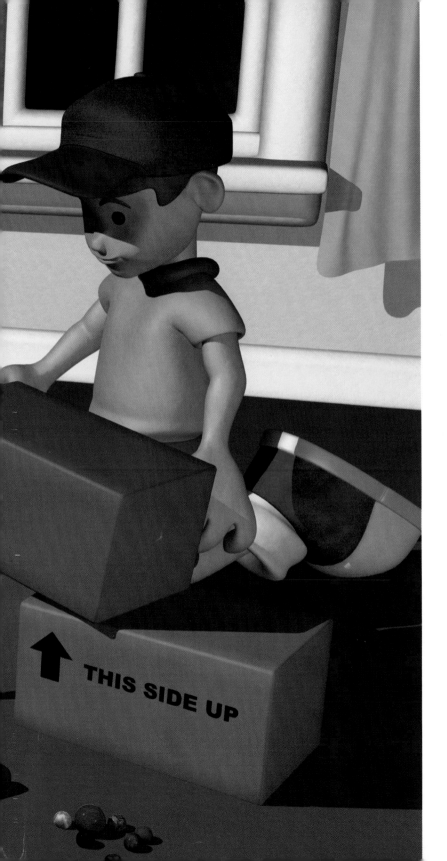

Happy and Max love
to build camps.

If building forts was
a contest, they would
be champs.

But Happy and Max
always built their
forts inside.

Camping outdoors was
something they had
never tried.

"Happy," Max said, "this tent, it's all right."

"But that tree house out there is where we should sleep tonight."

"We'll spend the night in the tree house, just you and me."

"We'll camp in the tree house. We'll like it. You'll see."

Happy and Max packed
their things for the night.

As they headed down-
stairs, Max tried out
their flashlight.

Across the backyard,
Happy and Max made
their way.

They walked toward
the great tree, where
tonight they would stay.

"Happy," Max said,
"tonight in this tree
house we'll camp out
for real."

"By tomorrow morning,
we'll know how true
campers feel."

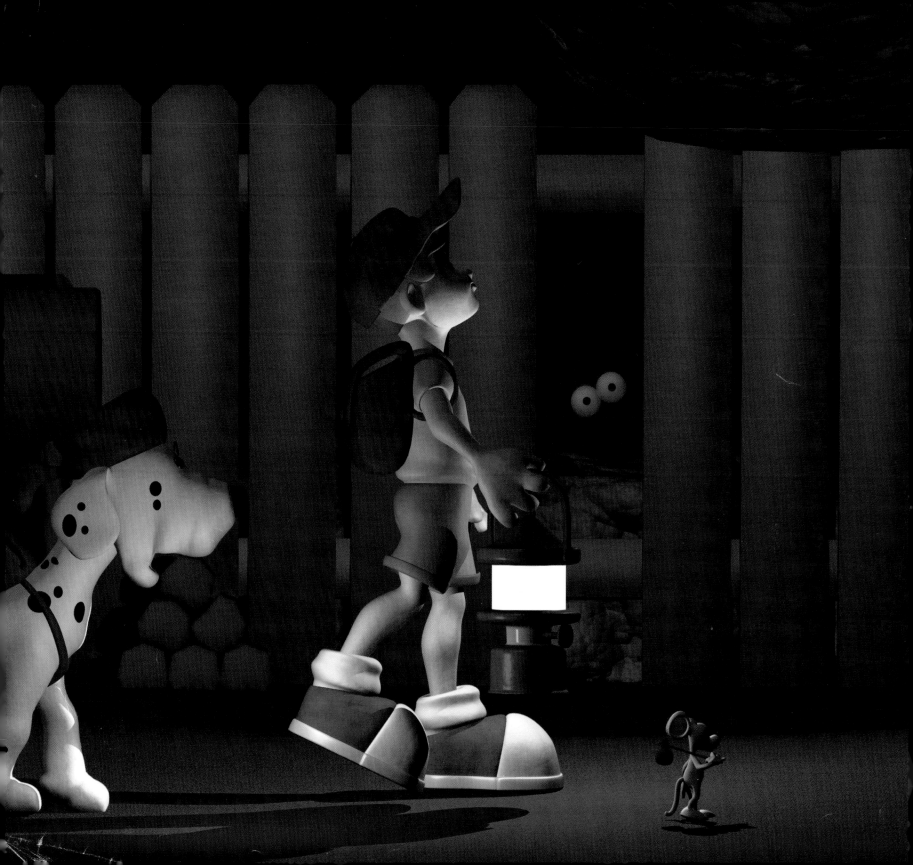

Max turned to Happy, as they approached the great tree.

"This will be our best fort yet, Happy. Just wait, you'll see."

"This tree house, people say, has been here for years."

"Real campers, like us Happy, don't have any fears."

Happy looked back at Max, not quite sure if he was right.

Happy had never been in a tree house before, much less spent the night.

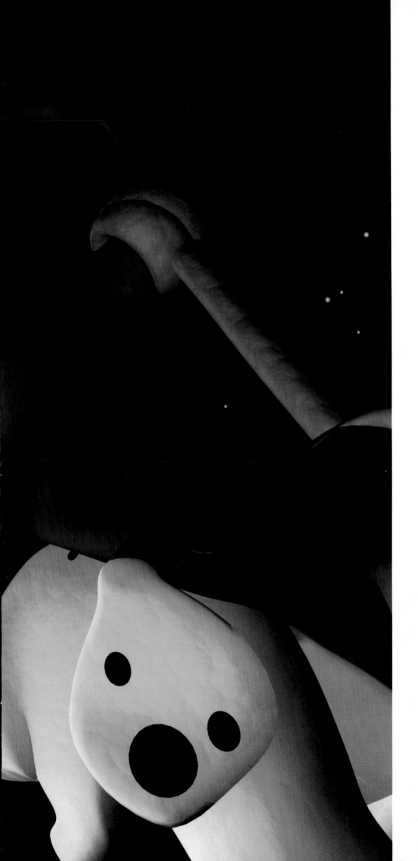

Max looked at the ladder, and then looked up the tree.

Sure the tree house looked high, but how high could it be?

Happy looked at the tree house, and to him it looked far.

"From that tree house," Happy thought, "I will look down on the moon, maybe even the stars."

"Come on, Happy,"
Max said, as he
climbed up the ladder.

But Happy stayed
where he was, until
Max asked, "Happy,
what's the matter?"

Try as he might,
Happy could not reach
the ladder's first rung.

"Surely, this means,"
Happy thought, "for
this tree house, I am
still too young."

"To sleep in a tree
house," thought Happy,
"I'm pretty sure that
one should be older."

Compared to his bed,
a tree house at night
would be darker and
much colder.

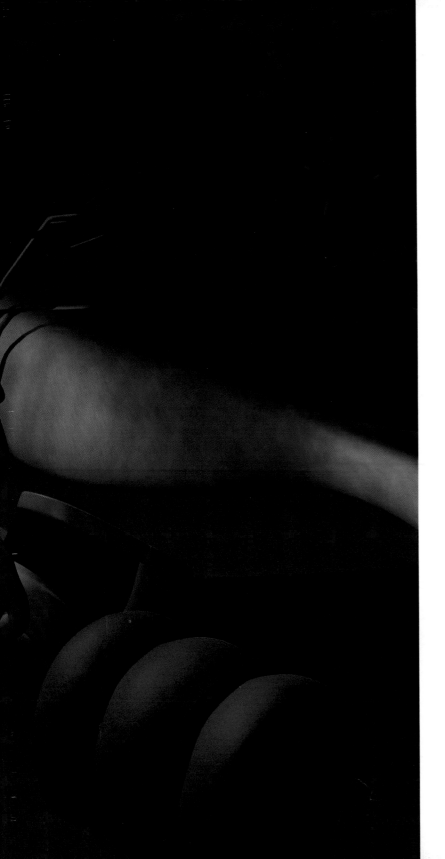

"Don't worry, Happy,"
Max said to his pal.

"We'll get you up in the
tree house. We'll figure
out how."

Max climbed back to the
ground and dumped out
his pack.

"Come on, Happy," said
Max, "you can ride on
my back."

"Happy," said Max,
"let's give it a try."

So they climbed up
the ladder, making
their way toward
the sky.

Happy had covered
his face as they
climbed away from
the ground.

"Happy," Max said,
"open your eyes and
take a look around."

Happy thought to
himself, "This just
doesn't seem right."

"A house in a tree is
no place for a dog
at night."

Happy and Max kept climbing, until they reached the tree house door.

"Thank goodness we've finally made it," thought Happy. "I could not take that climbing for very much more."

"Happy," Max said, "check out this place. Our very own tree house. Our very own space."

"Happy," said Max, "let's prepare for the night."

"We'll unpack our things."

"We'll set them up right."

Happy set out his things, and he brushed off his paws.

He fluffed up his pillows, and put on his pajamas.

"This won't be so bad," Happy thought, as he laid down.

"It's only a tree house and the tree touches the ground."

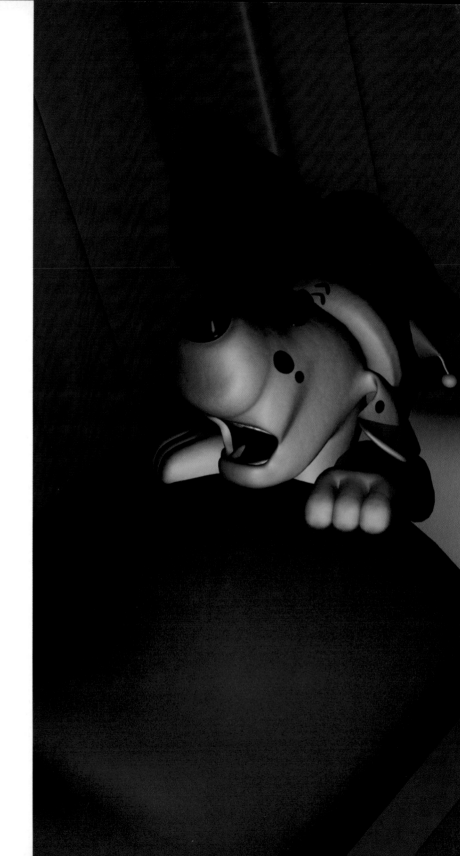

SPOOKY STORIES

BY ART VANDELEIGH

Max reached into
his pack and he pulled
out two books.

"Look, Happy!" Max
said, "I've brought
camping stories, with
witches, ghosts, and
spooks."

As Max read the
first story, Happy
thought the tree
house seemed larger.

As the moon moved
behind the clouds,
Happy knew the tree
house was darker.

Happy felt worried,
but he tried to hide
his fright.

"Happy," Max said,
"things are going to
be all right."

"We'll be safe in this
tree house, and it's
just for one night."

"And besides, Happy,"
said Max, "if it gets
any darker, I'll turn
on our flashlight."

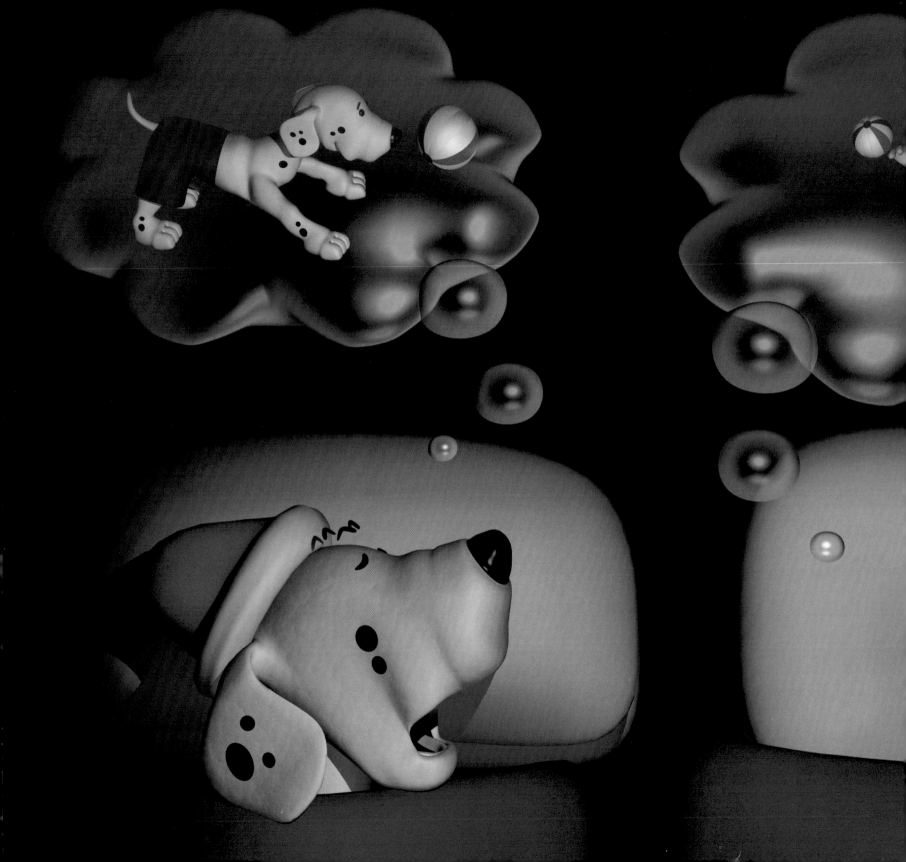

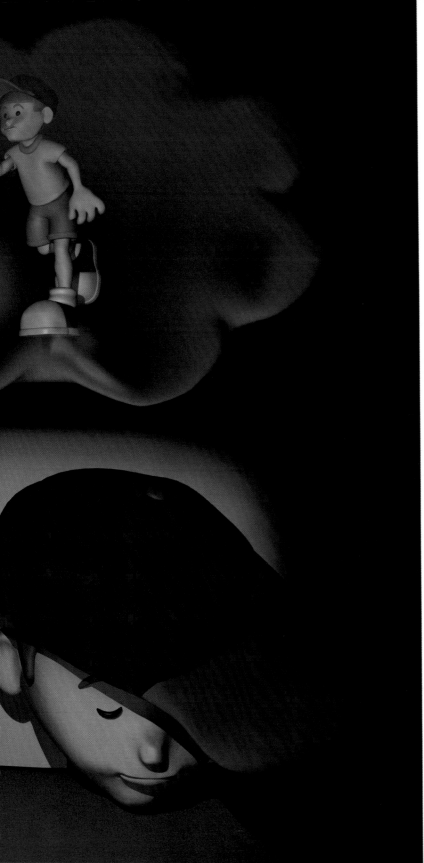

"Finally," Happy thought, as Max finished the last story.

"I can go to sleep now and wake up in the morning."

Happy and Max snuggled deep in their beds.

Soon both were asleep, with dreams filling their heads.

But in the tree house
that night, not everyone
was sleeping.

Thunk,

Clunk,

Clang,

Bang!

Hearing the loud
noises, Happy and
Max sat straight up
in bed.

"Ouch!" said Happy,
"something hit me on
the head!"

"Happy," Max shouted,
"hand me the light."

"We're not alone in
this tree house. There's
someone else here
tonight."

Happy stood close to
Max and the light lit
up their space.

"I liked it much better,"
Happy thought, "when we
were alone in this place."

"Happy," said Max,
"those were just camping
noises. Don't be afraid."

Happy wished, however,
that it was back in their
bedroom they had stayed.

Max rose from his
bed and grabbed his
knapsack.

Happy, remembering
the ladder, jumped into
Max's pack.

"Don't be afraid," Happy
repeated to himself.

"That noise we just
heard was just a tree
house sound."

As Max held up the
lantern, Happy, feeling
braver, began to look
around.

"Agggggghhh!" barked
Happy. "Agggggghhh!"

"Max! A monster!"
Happy barked. "Max!
It's behind us!"

"Turn around, Max!
It's a tree house
monster!"

Max turned around
quickly, ready to
meet the monster
face to face.

But the monster was
gone.

It had disappeared
without a trace.

"Aggggghhh!" Happy
barked. "

The monster is in front
of me now!"

"Max! The monster is
bigger!"

"Get us out of here
somehow!"

With Happy in his backpack, Max rushed across the tree house floor.

Max unlocked the latch and climbed out through the door.

Happy closed his eyes
as they climbed down
the tree.

To be back in his own
bed, that's where Happy
wanted to be.

Happy opened one eye
and looked back up
the tree.

If the monster was
coming, Happy would
help Max get free.

Max ran with Happy,
away from the great
tree.

Away from the monster,
that only Happy could
see.

Max ran across the yard
toward their back door.

But Happy was heavy,
and soon Max could not
run any more.

Max, tired from running,
stopped and looked all
around.

Max looked back behind
them, and then he looked
at the ground.

Suddenly Max chuckled,
and soon he bent over
with laughter.

"Happy," Max said, "let
me introduce you to your
monster."

"Happy," said Max, as he
made the flashlight glow,
"the monster you fear
is just your shadow."

Happy, feeling pretty
silly, was glad that Max
was right.

"Come on, Happy, old
buddy," Max said,
"let's call it a night."

And they headed into
their house, to Happy's
delight.

Playing the Happy and Max Adventure Using Your Car Stereo or Audio-CD Player

To play the Happy and Max adventure using your car stereo or audio-CD player, simply insert the CD into your audio-CD player. Next, use your player's Seek button to advance to track 2 (the programs for your PC reside on track 1) and then press the Play button.

The audio CD assigns a track number to each page of the book. So, if you must stop and later restart the CD, you can use your player's Seek button to advance to the track where you left off.

Loading the Adventure Under Windows®95 or Higher

Insert the Kids Interactive CD into your PC's CD-ROM drive. Your system, in turn, should automatically start the Happy and Max adventure program, displaying the program's main menu on your screen.

If your program does not start after you insert the CD, use your word processor or the Windows Notepad accessory to open the Readme file which resides on the CD-ROM. The Readme file will walk you through steps you can perform to run the program.

Loading the Adventure on a Mac

Insert the Kids Interactive CD into your Mac's CD-ROM drive. Your system, in turn, should display a CD-ROM icon on your desktop. Double click your mouse on the CD-ROM icon and open the Tree House folder. Within the folder, double click your mouse on the Tree House program icon to run the program.

Troubleshooting the Happy and Max CD-ROM

If you have trouble loading the Happy and Max adventure, use your word processor to open the Readme file which resides on the Happy and Max CD-ROM. The Readme file contains steps you can perform to run the program. In addition, you'll find more troubleshooting tips at the Happy and Max Web site at www.HappyAndMax.com.

Starting Your Adventure

After you load and run the Happy and Max adventure, your computer's screen will display the program's main menu as shown in Figure 1.

Figure 1 The Happy and Max main menu.

From within the main menu, you can start the interactive book, access the CD's two adventure games, or exit the program. In addition, the main menu provides an on-line help button, which will further explain how you can use the CD. To select an option within the main menu, click your mouse on the option's paw prints.

Reading Along with the Interactive CD

The Happy and Max CD-ROM contains an interactive version of the Happy and Max adventure. Within the interactive story, a narrator will read the story as the images appear on your computer screen. After the narrator stops reading the text, move your mouse within the image. When your mouse pointer changes from an arrow to a pointing hand, click your mouse button. You have found one of the story's interactive elements.

Depending on the element, your PC may show a close-up image of the object, play an audio file, or both. To resume the story, simply click your mouse a second time within the image.

To move from one page to the next within the story, click your mouse on the Next button. To move back to the previous page, click your mouse on the Back button.

Playing the Interactive Games

Each CD-ROM in the Happy and Max Adventure series includes two interactive computer games. To play the games, click your mouse on the main menu Play the Games option. The program, in turn, will display the Games Menu, as shown in Figure 2, from which you can choose the game you want to play.

Figure 2 The Happy and Max Games menu.

To play a game, click your mouse on the button that appears beneath the game you desire. Happy and Max The Night in the Tree House includes a shadow matching game and a pong game.

How Do I Use the Interactive CD-ROM?

 Ignore the CD and simply read the book

 Each CD provides two interactive games

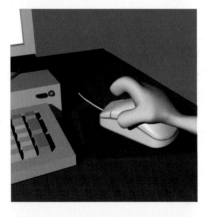 Interact with the story using a PC (running Windows 95 or higher) or a Mac

 Put the CD in your stereo and listen while you read

 Take the CD with you in the car and listen while you read

kids interactive™

...a young reader's best friend™